This Little Tiger Book belongs to:

_____

_____

_____

_____

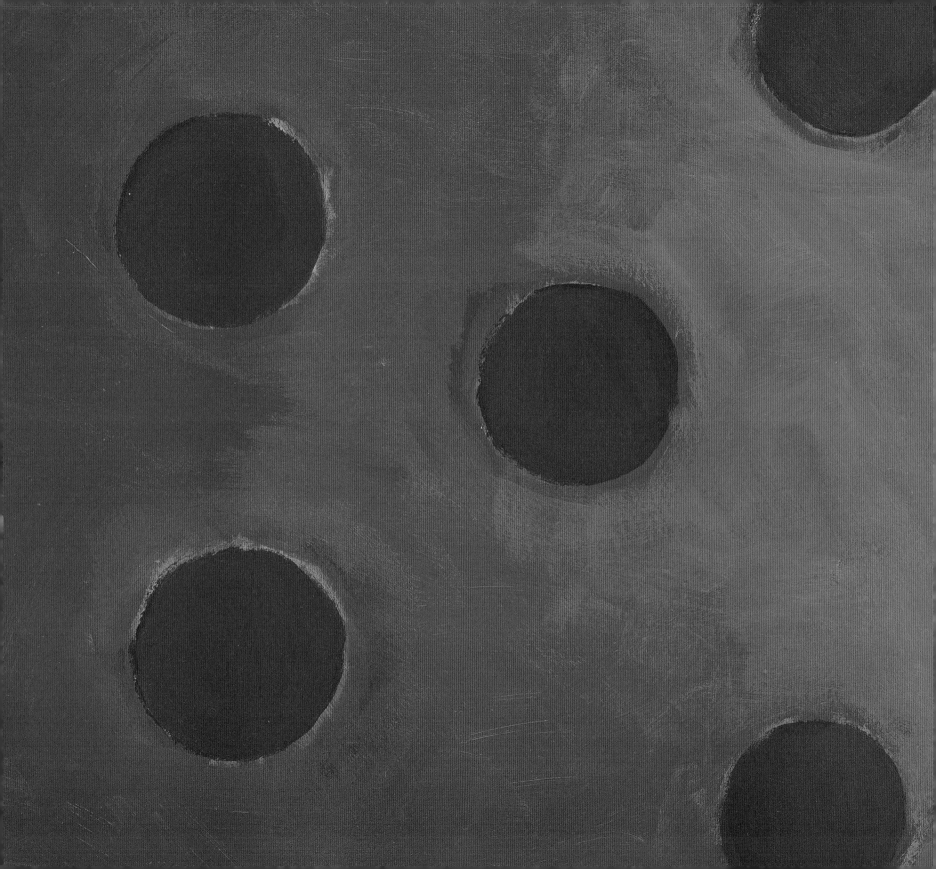

For Andrea & Claudia
— I F

For Mum & Dad, who helped
— J T

LITTLE TIGER PRESS
1 The Coda Centre, 189 Munster Road, London SW6 6AW
www.littletigerpress.com

First published in Great Britain 1999
This edition published 1999

A CIP catalogue record for this book is
available from the British Library

All rights reserved • ISBN 978-1-85430-628-9

Printed in China • LTP/1400/0446/0512

14 16 18 20 19 17 15 13

The Very Lazy Ladybird

by Isobel Finn & Jack Tickle

LITTLE TIGER PRESS
London

This is the story of
a very lazy ladybird.

She liked to sleep all day . . .

and all night.

And because she slept
all day and all night,
this lazy ladybird didn't
know how to fly.

One day the lazy
ladybird wanted to
sleep somewhere else.
But what could she do
if she couldn't fly?

Then the lazy
ladybird had
a very good
idea.

she hopped into her pouch.

But the kangaroo liked to

JUMP!

"I can't sleep in here," cried the lazy ladybird. "It's far too bumpy."

So when a tiger padded by . . .

she hopped onto his back.

But the tiger liked to

ROAR!

"I can't sleep here,"
said the lazy ladybird.
"It's far too noisy."

So when a crocodile swam by . . .

she hopped onto his tail.

But the crocodile liked to

SWISH

his tail in the water.

"I can't sleep here," said the lazy ladybird. "I'll fall into the river!"

So when a monkey swung by . . .

she hopped onto her head.

But the monkey liked to

SWING

from branch to branch.

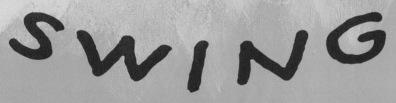

"I can't sleep here," said the lazy ladybird. "I'm feeling dizzy."

So when a bear ambled by . . .

she hopped onto his ear.

But the bear
liked to

SCRATCH!

"I can't sleep here,"
said the lazy ladybird.
"He'll never sit still."

So when a tortoise plodded by . . .

she hopped onto her shell.

But the tortoise liked to

S N O O Z E

in the sun.
"I can't sleep here,"
said the lazy ladybird.
"It's far too hot."

So when an elephant trundled by . . . .

she hopped onto his trunk.

"At last!" thought
the lazy ladybird.
"I've found
someone
who doesn't . . .

jump . . .

But at that very moment . . .

the elephant

HOOo

and poor old lazy ladybird . . .

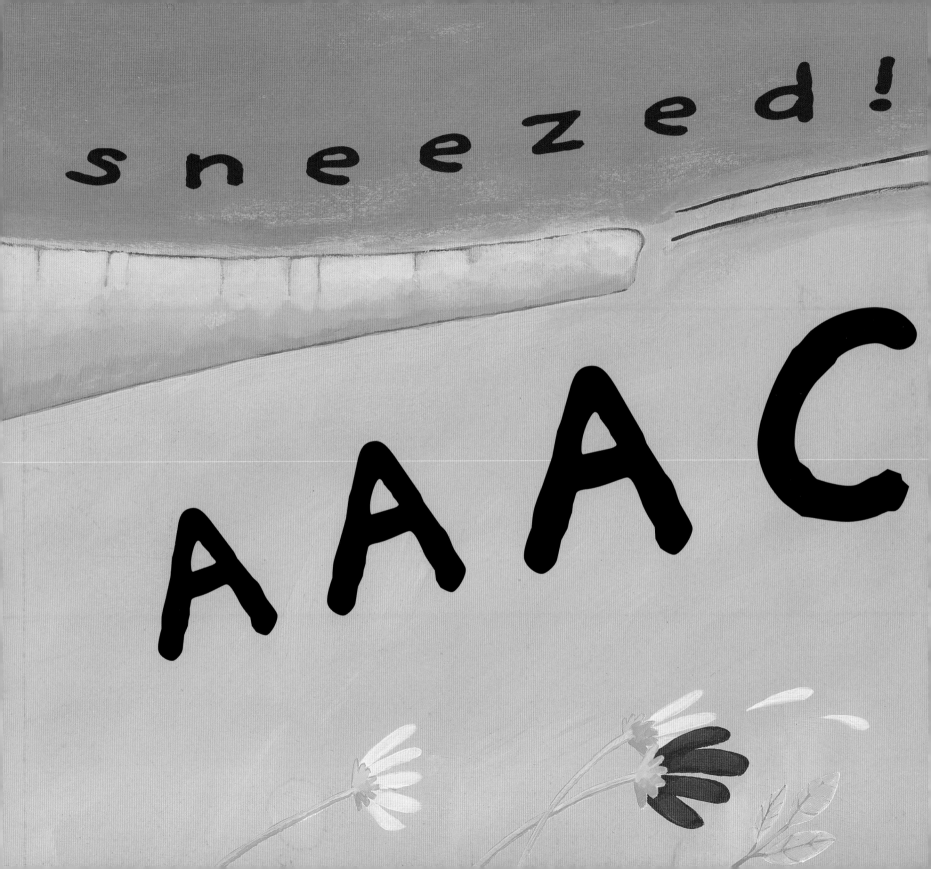

had to fly at last!

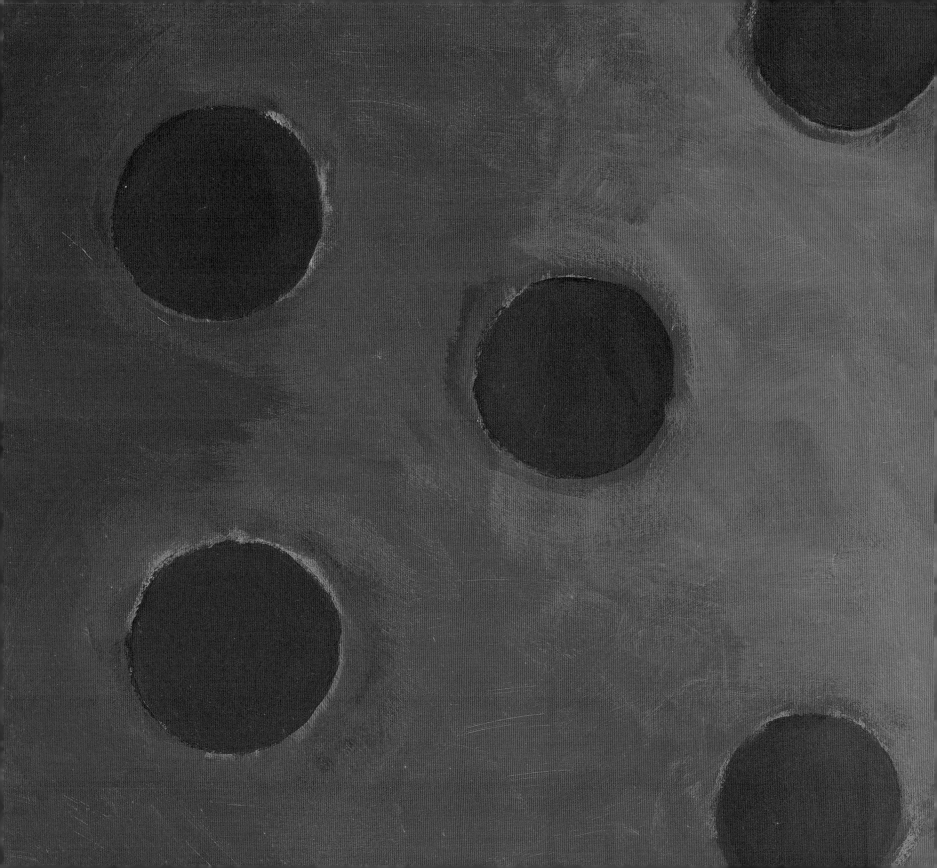

Spot the latest books
from Little Tiger Press

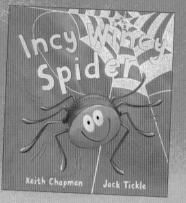
Incy Wincy Spider
Keith Chapman | Jack Tickle

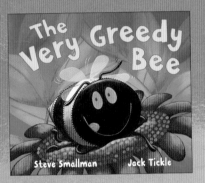
The Very Greedy Bee
Steve Smallman | Jack Tickle

The Crunching Munching Caterpillar
Sheridan Cain
Jack Tickle

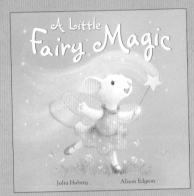
A Little Fairy Magic
Julia Hubery | Alison Edgson

Can You See SASSOON?
Sam Usher

Oh Dylan!
Tracey Corderoy | Tina Macnaughton

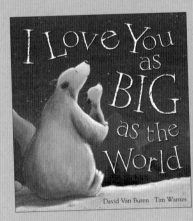
I Love You as BIG as the World
David Van Buren | Tim Warnes

For information regarding any of the above titles or
for our catalogue, please contact us:

Little Tiger Press
1 The Coda Centre
189 Munster Road
London SW6 6AW
Tel: 020 7385 6333
Fax: 020 7385 7333
Email: info@littletiger.co.uk
www.littletigerpress.com